RABBIT SCHOOL

A Light-Hearted Tale

verse by ALBERT SIXTUS

illustrations by

FRITZ KOCH-GOTHA

translated from the German by

Roland Freischlad

DAVID R. GODINE · PUBLISHER · BOSTON

"Blow your nose and use a leaf
   As your cabbage-handkerchief,"
   Mother Bunny says. "And, look
   After your own slate and book!
   And be sure your sponge is wet!
   Have you washed your paws just yet?
   Good. And now you're off to class."
"Mommy … Bye!" say lad and lass.

Bunny Hans and Bunny Gretchen,
Paw in paw, they look so fetching.
Happily they skip along
With the gath'ring bunny throng
Which they meet along the way.
Almost seven! Don't delay!
Each one's backpack, dark or pale,
Bounces o'er a bunny tail.

Take a leap so you can cross
Over to the dark green moss!
Further, by the pines and brook,
Nestled in a meadow nook
Lies the rabbit school, you see:
Benches spaced in rows of three.
Here now, take one final hop,
At your seats it's time to stop!

Soon the janitor, Stillwell,
Goes to ring the morning bell.
Then, amid the children's cheers,
The school's teacher now appears.
He wears glasses, has a beard,
And long ears – he is revered.
"Close your eyes and fold your hands,
Till the morning prayer ends!"

Now they tackle their first hour,
Study many a plant and flower;
Answering, as you just saw,
After lifting up a paw!
Then the teacher, with crossed feet,
Asks which plants are good to eat.
Bunny Hans, he can attest
"Cabbage tastes by far the best."

Next they face the second hour
With a subject mighty dour.
Of the wicked fox they're reading,
They discuss his ways misleading:
How he scurries – rush, rush, rush –
O'er the fields and through the brush.
Little Gretel has one thought:
"I must simply not be caught!"

Easter eggs of ev'ry color
Brighten rabbit eyes once duller.
Each one takes an egg, still white,
Picks a brush – with touch so light –
And then paints with craft and skill,
Learns their calling to fulfill.
If their colors are too runny,
They won't be an Easter Bunny!

Finally, here comes the break.
"Not too wild, for goodness' sake!"
Once outdoors, boys run and jump,
Over every root and stump.
Look, the girls … they like to walk
With their girlfriends, and to talk,
As they nibble and they gnaw
On vegetables, fresh and raw.

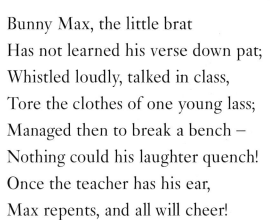

Bunny Max, the little brat
Has not learned his verse down pat;
Whistled loudly, talked in class,
Tore the clothes of one young lass;
Managed then to break a bench –
Nothing could his laughter quench!
Once the teacher has his ear,
Max repents, and all will cheer!

Bunny Minnie, out to win,
Brings the teacher's violin.
He, in turn, prepares the bow,
Tunes the strings, some high, some low.
Ping, pang, pung... It's sounding right,
And the teacher with delight
Takes the fiddle to his chin:
Let the rabbit songs begin.

Look, the bunny lads are rushing
With the water cans. "No sloshing!"
Since the cabbage leaves are wilting,
Every boy a can is tilting.
Bunny lasses see the need,
Start at once the fields to weed.
And the teacher, can't you tell:
He makes sure that all goes well!

In the morning's final hour –
It is Sports – they run full power.
Here they learn how to escape
From the dogs that are in shape!
That's a game of life and death –
Hopeless, if you're out of breath!
Here they learn to "zig" and "zag"
To make sure they dodge attack.

F. Koch-Gotha - 23

Finally, the teacher pleads:
"Please, leave nothing in your seats!
Home you go! Do not delay!
And be quiet on the way!
Stay alert and look around,
Do not leave familiar ground!
When the fox snaps at your heel,
Don't become the villain's meal!"

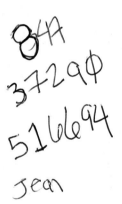

Can you hear those wily whimpers
With a voice that slyly simpers:
"Help me, bunnies, over here!"
Says that rascal, "Have no fear!"
Is this not the cunning fox,
With those eyes like fiery rocks?
Run, you bunnies, like the wind,
And escape that dreaded fiend!

Well now, rabbit school is out,
And at home there is a stout
Lunch prepared for lad and lass,
Made of cabbage and of cress.
With their fork and with a will
They intend to eat their fill!
If I weren't a kid, I'd be
A bunny, most undoubtedly!

First U.S. edition published in 2009 by
David R. Godine · Publisher
Post Office Box 450
Jaffrey, New Hampshire 03452
www.godine.com

FIRST U.S. EDITION
Printed in Belgium